To William

First published 2010 by Walker Books Ltd, 87 Vauxhall Walk, London SE11 5HJ

10 9 8 7 6 5 4 3 2 1

© 2010 Petr Horáček

The right of Petr Horáček to be identified as author/illustrator of this work has been asserted by him in accordance with the Copyright, Designs and Patents Act 1988

This book has been typeset in Little Grog

Printed in Thailand

British Library Cataloguing in Publication Data:
a catalogue record for this book is available from the British Library

ISBN 978-1-4063-1392-5

www.walker.co.uk

The Fly

Petr Horáček

WALKER BOOKS
AND SUBSIDIARIES
LONDON • BOSTON • SYDNEY • AUCKLAND

Two goggly eyes,
six hairy legs,
two transparent wings...

It's ME!
The House Fly.
But people don't like me
being in the house.

After breakfast I do my exercises... 156 times around

the lamp keeps me fit.

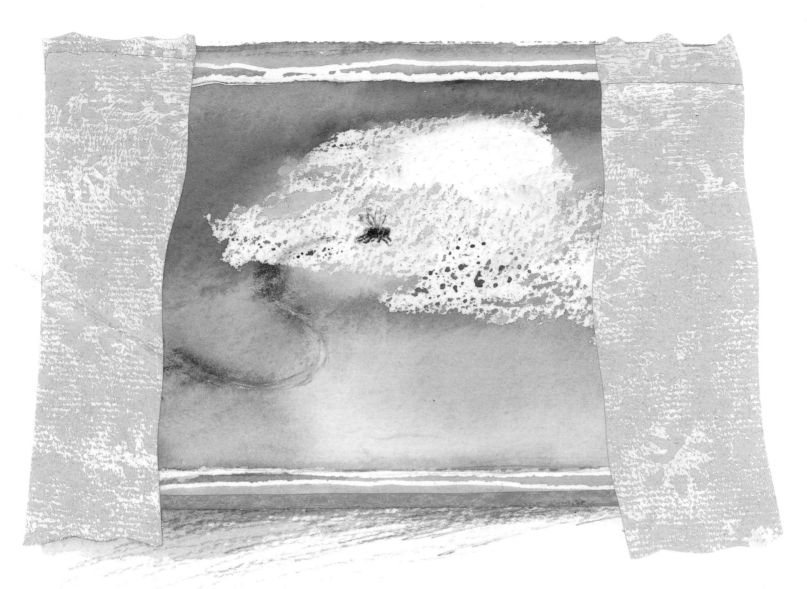

Then it's time for a snack.
I don't mind sharing, but he
doesn't want to share with me.
Flap! That was close!

But the animals don't really like me. I don't know why.

Once a frog nearly ate me,

then a bird nearly caught me.

Both in the same day.
Why?

I go back to the House for lunch.
I like my meals on time!

I can never understand ...

FLAP!

FLAP!

FLAP!

what the fuss is about.

FLAP!

Even when I find a good place to rest.

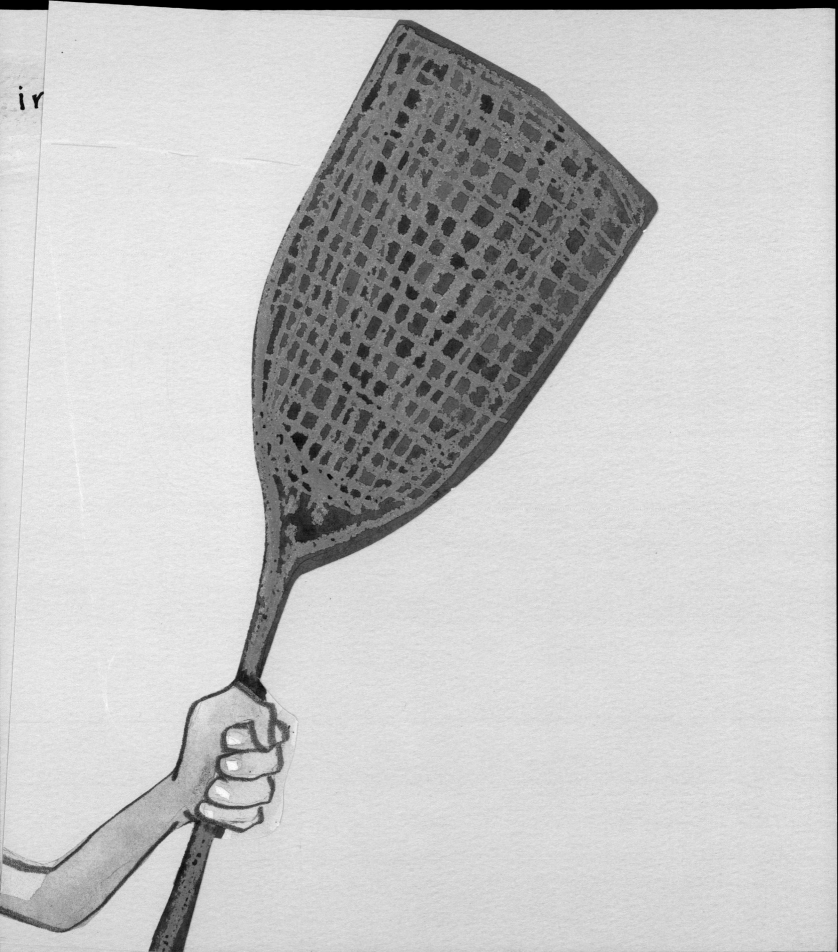